KOTUKU
The flight of the white heron

STORY BY
PHILIP TEMPLE

ILLUSTRATED BY
CHRIS GASKIN

Hodder & Stoughton
A member of the Hodder Headline Group

One early summer, long ago, Mata was hatched among bottlebrush flowers in a land of paperbark trees. She had a hard time surviving in her nest because she had to compete for food with two stronger male chicks. But her feathers grew fast and after she saw her second full moon she stretched her wings with the urge to fly.

First she learned to balance on her long legs as she flapped to the top of her nesting tree. She almost tipped over. But from there she could see all the great swamp, shimmering in the summer heat.

Around her were hundreds of other herons. Ibises and cormorants nested there, too. They had different ways of living and fishing. But to Mata they were as familiar as the reflections of clouds in water and the sharpness of the claws on her long toes.

After much practice, and one or two crashes, Mata was strong enough to leave her parents and fly away to feed. Summer rains and flooding rivers had filled the swamp and made it rich with fish and frogs. She had to share these with many other kinds of birds, such as swamp hens and pelicans and swans. But she soon found the feeding places which suited her best.

Then the rain went away and the rivers dropped and the swamp began to dry up in the heat. Food became scarce and Mata grew hungry. When she saw most of the other herons leaving, she also flew away to find a new feeding place far from her crowded home.

Mata strengthened her wings in long searching flights. She tested the waters of billabongs and rivers. She tried lakes and marshes. But the place she liked most was a lagoon she discovered behind a long beach. When the sea flooded through the mangroves twice each day, she was able to catch lots of prawns and bream, young mullet and silver biddy. She grew fat and her feathers began to shine.

Early one morning Mata caught a mullet that was too big to swallow in one gulp. A prowling sea eagle spotted her struggles and dived down to attack. It slashed at her neck with its talons and snatched at the fish with its hooked beak.

Mata flew fast and high in fright and the fish fell from her beak as greedy gulls attacked her, too. She fled towards the safety of the empty, open sea.

Mata flew strongly until all the attacking birds were far behind. The fresh wind helped her, taking hold of her broad wings and lifting her higher than she had ever flown before.

When Mata felt safe, she turned to fly back to the mangroves. But the wind had suddenly grown stronger than the power in her wings. She became alarmed when, no matter how hard she flew, the land grew more and more distant.

Faster and faster she drifted, blown away from the lagoon that had become her home. Soon the land disappeared behind cold grey clouds. Soon she could see nothing but endless grey waves rolling towards the edge of the world.

Mata flew with the strong wind through a star-filled night and into another day. She became hungry, but there was nowhere for her to stand and hunt for fish among the crests of the stormy sea. To save energy, she used her wings just enough to keep aloft. Even so, she felt her strength slowly fading away.

Late on the second day she saw the waves ending. They broke against an endless beach. Behind the beach was a strange forest, dark in the evening light. And behind the darkness were high mountains whose frozen rivers reflected the colour of the setting sun. Mata glided down to rest at last.

Mata was starving after her long flight and she had lost all her fat. At the entrance to a big lagoon she stood hungrily in the shallow waters and fished all day for tiny silvery-white fish, stabbing at them as they swam past.

At first, Mata was not always successful at fishing for the strange animals in this new lagoon. But with practice she grew better and began to catch plenty of small eels, shrimps and large insects, too.

When she had recovered from her long, exhausting flight Mata explored the coast and forested plains of the new land. She found it colder and wetter than the one she had grown up in. But there were many swamps, lakes and rivers where she could feed.

The land was filled with trees and plants that Mata had never seen before. Most of the birds were strange to her and there were no other white herons. But she was so busy exploring and catching food that she did not miss the company of her own kind.

Many of the strangers were unable to fly and the most enormous birds she had ever seen stalked along the forest edge. One attacked her while she fished in a lake and she was forced to fly into the trees to escape its snapping, rapping beak.

At the big lagoon, during her third winter in the new land, long feathers began to grow from Mata's back. They were as fine as plumes of toe toe. She felt different and wanted to display herself to other white herons. When the kowhai trees bloomed, Mata started to fly back to the far-off swamp where she had been hatched.

Mata knew which way to fly. And she knew how long it would take her. But she spent months trying to find a place from where the winds would help to carry her over the ocean. She even reached the end of the new land, where there was nothing but sand and sea.

Every time she tried, the wind blew against her. Slowly she became exhausted and lost the urge to fly home. Mata's plumes fell to earth like pale discarded leaves. Again she wandered alone.

In the next winter, as she hunted in the deep south, her plumes appeared again and grew longer and longer. When the clematis flowered over the beech trees, she again felt the need to fly home. But this time she flew back to the big lagoon which she now felt was home in the land that was no longer new to her.

When Mata reached the big lagoon she saw a white figure perched in a tall kahikatea tree. It was a bird that, for almost three years, she had seen only as a reflection of herself in the waters where she fished.

The new white heron was a male who had also wind-drifted across the sea. Mata could see others scattered like flowers over the dark green swamp forest. But Puaho was the only one who wore long plumes like hers. Mata clattered her beak in excitement. Her long and lonely journeys were ended.

Puaho fanned his plumes and raised his beak to the sky. Then he raised his wing and ran his beak along its edge. Puaho and Mata displayed and danced for each other. Their eyes and faces, their beaks and their legs had changed to the colour of mating.

Puaho chose a nesting place in the crest of riverside trees near the big lagoon. He brought sticks for Mata who wriggled them into place with her beak. Each time Puaho arrived he called out to her — grock-grock-grock. And they lifted their plumes and stretched out their necks and heads in greeting.

Mata laid three eggs and she and Puaho kept them warm until they hatched a month later. By that time, their mating colours had disappeared. Puaho and Mata also took turns to feed their chicks until they had learned to fly and care for themselves. By the end of the long breeding season, Mata and Puaho had become thin and tired.

The family of herons left their nesting tree and wandered far across the country, each finding their own feeding places for the autumn and winter.

No matter how far Mata and Puaho travelled, they always returned to their nesting tree near the big lagoon in spring.

After their second return a terrible storm raged in from the sea. Branches were torn from the trees and the herons were unable to find food for their young. Mata and Puaho lost their new brood of chicks before any were strong enough to fly.

But they did not give up. They returned year after year. They hatched more young birds and when these grew old enough, they mated and hatched their own. The colony grew and grew until there were more than fifty noisy nests each spring.

Even now, after wandering the land in autumn and winter, white herons still return each spring to the trees not far from the big lagoon. Each year they grow delicate plumes. Each year their eyes and beaks and faces and legs change to the colours of mating. Each year they court and dance for each other. Each year the white herons build nests and raise their young in the same way that Mata and Puaho did after their long flights over the ocean, thousands of years ago.

FACTS ABOUT THE WHITE HERON

The white heron is one of the most common birds in the world. It is found throughout southern Europe, central and east Asia, Africa, North and South America and Australia where it is known as the white egret or great egret. This name comes from aigrette, a French word used to describe the white heron's long mating plumes. From this comes its scientific name, *Egretta alba modesta*. It grows to about 100 cm tall, has a wingspan of about 150 cm and weighs around one kilogram.

The white heron is not common in New Zealand because it is at the limit of its southern hemisphere range. It breeds only beside the Waitangiroto River, north of Okarito Lagoon in South Westland. No-one knows when the first white herons arrived but fossil bones show they must have first wind-drifted across the Tasman Sea several thousand years ago.

The Maori named the white heron kotuku. It was seen so infrequently by them that it was used in proverb to describe a visitor who comes only rarely – He kotuku rerenga tahi i te tau. The kotuku was sacred to the Maori and its precious plumes were kept in special carved boxes, papa hou, when they were not being worn by rangatira. In this story we gave our birds Maori names. Mata means fresh growth and Puaho means intensely white.

The diagrams on the following pages serve as keys to the colour illustrations in this book.

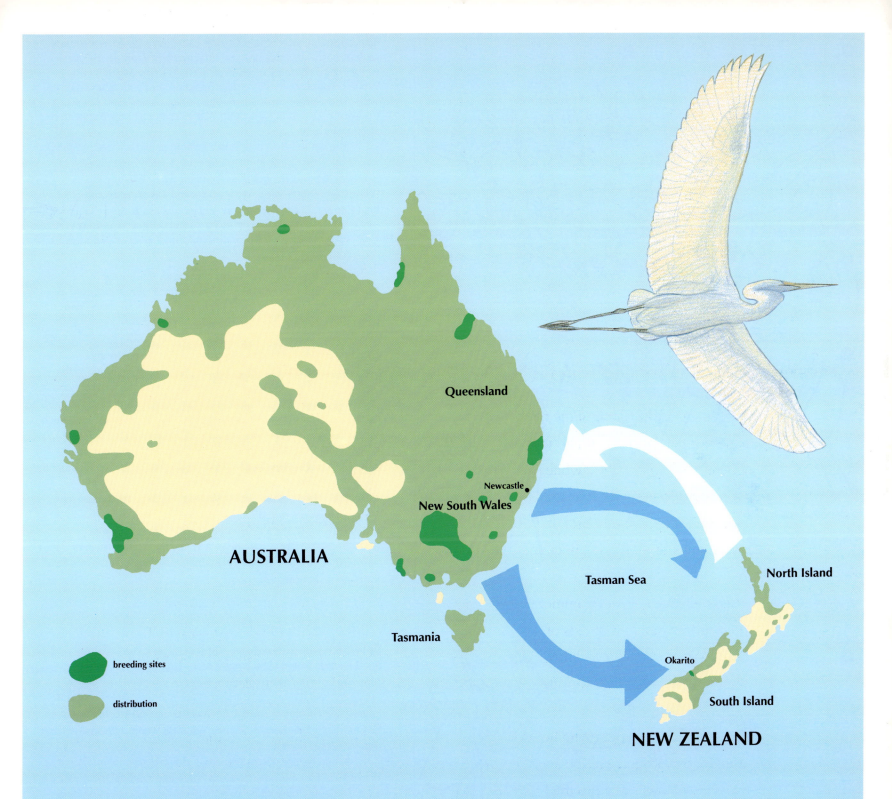

This map shows where the white heron lives and breeds in Australia and New Zealand and the possible flight paths that immigrant birds follow across the Tasman Sea.

1 In Australia, white herons – or great egrets – breed in wetlands such as freshwater swamps and tidal mangrove forests. The size of wetland bird colonies varies from 50 to as many as 3000 nests. White herons usually share their breeding sites with other colonial birds. This picture depicts a medium-sized colony (500 nests) in a freshwater swamp in New South Wales as it might have appeared 2000 years ago.

The white heron nest is in a swamp paperbark tree (*Melaleuca ericifolia*). Other birds in the picture are **1** Little Egret (*Egretta garzetta*). **2** Plumed Egret (*Egretta intermedia*). **3** White Ibis (*Threskiornis aethiopica*). **4** Straw-necked Ibis (*T. spinicollis*). **5** Little Pied Cormorant (*Phalacrocorax melanoleucos*). **6** Australian Pelican (*Pelecanus conspicillatus*). **7** Black Swan (*Cygnus atratus*). **8** Yellow-faced Honeyeater (*Lichenostomus chrysops*). **9** Scarlet Honeyeater (*Myzolema sanguinolenta*).

The New South Wales breeding season is normally between November and May when white herons lay as few as two and as many as six eggs. Young birds begin to scramble out of the nest when they are about five weeks old.

2 White herons make their first flight about six weeks after hatching. They practise flying for about ten days, returning to the nest to be fed by their parents, before they leave the nest for good. They feed mostly on aquatic animals such as fish and frogs, but also eat insects, snails, crustaceans such as shrimps and small birds such as silvereyes and sparrows. Water levels near breeding colonies must be sufficient to sustain aquatic life. If home wetland areas dry up then some or all white herons must disperse to find more favourable feeding grounds.

Other birds in the picture are **1** White Ibis. **2** Swamp Hen (*Porphyrio porphyrio*). **3** Dusky Moorhen (*Gallinula tenebrenosa*). **4** Black Swan. **5** Black Cormorant (*Phalacrocorax carbo*). **6** Chestnut Teal (*Anas castanea*). **7** White Eyed Duck (*Aythya australis*). A long-necked tortoise (*Cheladina longicollis*) peers from the water at bottom left.

3 White herons are known to disperse all over Australia in search of good feeding waters. The longest recorded movement by a single bird was from the Murrumbidgee River in southern New South Wales to New Guinea, a distance of more than 3200km. Coastal waters, such as this mangrove (*Avicennia marina*) lagoon, are often favoured by white herons because constant tidal waters guarantee a regular supply of food.

White herons normally feed on fish and other animals less than 12 cm long because they can catch and swallow them with ease. Difficulty in handling larger fish may encourage other birds to try and steal the prey. The large White-breasted Sea Eagle (*Haliaeetus leucogaster*) may also regard a white heron itself as prey.

4 The first flight of a white heron from Australia to New Zealand was probably accidental. It could have been caused by a disturbing incident — such as that shown in picture 3 — in combination with strong offshore winds and a favourable weather pattern which would help the bird to fly more than 2000 kms across the Tasman Sea. Westerly winds blowing from Australia to New Zealand are common around both high and low pressure systems. The first Tasman crossing by a group of white herons may have been caused by pressures such as drought or over-population which stimulated birds to seek new feeding grounds to the east.

This picture depicts the mouth of the Hunter Estuary in northern New South Wales 2000 years ago and shows Nobbys island connected by a narrow spit to the headland which is now part of the city of Newcastle.

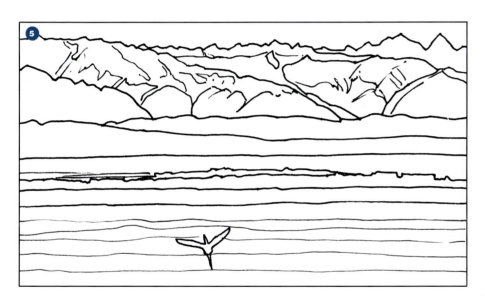

5 Studies of other birds on migration flights, such as the Australian cattle egret (*Ardeola ibis*) suggest that the most favourable altitude for birds crossing the Tasman Sea is between 1000 and 2000 metres above sea level. At that height following winds are likely to be steady and strong. The average flight speed of a heron on a long ocean crossing would be about 50 kilometres an hour. This assumes a good steady wind speed and the kind of 'flap and pause' flying technique a bird would use to conserve energy and fat reserves. A flight from the east coast of New South Wales to the west coast of the South Island would, therefore, take 40-45 hours.

The landfall of the white heron depicted is at Okarito Lagoon in South Westland. The Southern Alps with Mount Cook and the Franz Josef Glacier are shown in the background.

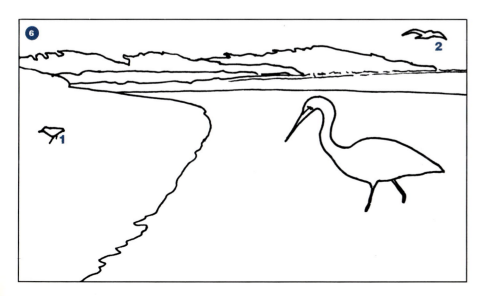

6 An important food for white herons in New Zealand is whitebait (*Galaxias attenuatus*) migrating into the tidal areas of lagoons and river estuaries. When fishing, a white heron stalks slowly through shallow water as it searches for food. When ready to attack, it draws back its head, developing a kink in the neck, and then swiftly strikes forward to spear its prey. Its fishing success rate varies and can be as low as only 25% of strikes; but some birds catch prey at the rate of three a minute. White herons usually feed alone and will sometimes rob other birds, such as shags. In modern times, herons raid artificial ponds and tanks for prey such as goldfish.

Other birds shown in the picture are **1** Banded Dotterel (*Charadrius bicinctus*). **2** Black-backed Gull (*Larus dominicanus*).

7 This picture shows podocarp forest in Westland. At the time of the arrival of the first white herons in New Zealand, perhaps 2000 years ago, birdlife was still unaffected by the hunting activities of humans and the mammals, such as rats, which they brought with them. In a land without mammals, flightless birds thrived. The largest were the moa, of which there were 12 species. Here are shown three *Dinornis giganteus*.

A white heron becomes mature in its third year. The first sign that it is ready to mate is the appearance of long dorsal (back) plumes which trail up to 100mm beyond its tail, forming a fine filigree train. These are the plumes, or aigrettes, which were later so prized by Maori chiefs.

When the urge to mate occurs, white herons return to their home colonies to breed. Before the establishment of the colony beside the Waitangiroto River, north of Okarito Lagoon, it is likely that the first white herons tried to recross the Tasman Sea to their home colonies in Australia.

8 To make a successful crossing from east to west, a bird must find an easterly airflow around the top of an anticyclone. The best are those centred near the middle of New Zealand which give migrants a good following wind after taking off from the upper part of the North Island. Today, cattle egrets, which breed in Australia, regularly visit New Zealand for the winter. They often use a southern flight path from Tasmania to the South Island, pushed by westerly winds; and a northern flight path from Northland to New South Wales, pushed by easterlies. In the 1950s large numbers of white herons reached New Zealand from Australia in autumn but decreased population numbers in the following springs gave evidence of trans-Tasman migration in both directions. For navigation, birds have an inherited or learned ability to use 'sun compasses' and to sense impulses from the earth's magnetic fields.

This picture shows Parengarenga Harbour in Northland with birds such as godwits which migrate to the Arctic at the onset of the New Zealand winter.

9 Before copulation and egg-laying, white herons undergo elaborate advertising and courtship behaviour. First, males attract females to a nesting site with a variety of displays which include neck hunching, extending neck and beak skywards, fanning plumes and flying in wide circles around the nest site.

Courtship begins aggressively and includes 'snap' and 'sneak' displays in which the males erect their nuptial plumes, stretch their necks high in the air and snap their bills. They preen their wings and take hold of twigs with their beaks, shaking them vigorously.

Birds reinforce their pair bonding with mutual preening and intertwining of necks, wings and bills. Sometimes, mates face each other with necks raised in an 'S' shape, plumes raised, and gently open and shut their beaks while in contact.

Before courtship, an adult white heron's bill changes colour, from yellow to purplish black; its facial skin changes from yellow to a bluish green; its eyes from yellow to red; its upper legs from black to black with a purple bloom.

10 Greeting displays and calls continue as the male brings twigs and fronds for the female to construct a sturdy nest about half a metre in diameter. At the Waitangiroto colony, nests are built in mahoe or pigeonwood trees or in the crowns of fern trees, 3-13 metres above the water. Three to five eggs are laid in late September or October, incubated by both parents, and they hatch in about 25 days. The young are fed by regurgitation. They begin to clamber from the nest after three weeks and are fledged after a further three weeks. The breeding season at Waitangiroto is normally completed by New Year when both parents and young birds disperse to feed throughout New Zealand until the start of the next breeding season in September.

11 The Waitangiroto colony is less than two kilometres from the Tasman Sea. It is vulnerable to disruption from storms in early spring which can make adequate feeding of chicks difficult. Success in fledging consequently varies from year to year. The persistence of white herons in returning to this colony site is undoubtedly related to the spring-rich feeding grounds of Okarito Lagoon, a few kilometres to the south, which is the largest of Westland's tidal estuaries. Surrounding swamps and rivers also help to protect the Waitangiroto colony from predators.

The fact that no other breeding colonies exist, and that the New Zealand resident population does not exceed 140, is evidence that the white heron is living and breeding at its climatic limit. In the northern hemisphere it also does not favour cool temperate regions.

12 The Waitangiroto colony was known to the Maori but was not discovered by Europeans until 1865. Vandalism in the 1870s almost destroyed the colony, only six pairs being counted in 1877. Sawmilling became a threat in the 20th century so that a 60m sanctuary strip was proclaimed in 1924 and a 773-hectare reserve in 1957. This special nature sanctuary has now increased in size to 1534 hectares and entry is by permit only. There is no evidence to indicate how many nests the colony supported in pre-human times. Annual records have been kept since 1941 when only four nests were active. Today, the colony supports an average of 50 nests and more than 60 chicks have been successfully reared in a season.

Fossil records indicate that, between 1000 and 6000 years ago, there could have been breeding colonies at Tom Bowling Bay, near North Cape, and at Poukawa and Te Aute in Hawkes Bay.

Two other birds have a special relationship with the white herons at Waitangiroto — **1** the Little Shag (*Phalacrocorax melanoleucos*) and **2** the Royal Spoonbill (*Platalea leucorodia*). A common colonial neighbour of white herons in Australia, there were only occasional records of spoonbills reaching New Zealand before the 1930s. The first breeding pair were seen at Waitangiroto in 1949 and they have nested there regularly since. Subsequently they have established breeding colonies at Wairau Lagoon, Marlborough and on Maukiekie and Green islands, off the Otago Coast.

IMMIGRANT BIRDS

Many of New Zealand's endemic and native birds began life in this country as immigrants from Australia and the south-west Pacific. Some, such as the parrot species which developed into both the kea (*Nestor notabilis*) and the kaka (*Nestor meridionalis*), arrived here so long ago — tens of thousands of years — that these birds now have no close relatives in other countries.

Species which arrived more recently are identical, or very similar, to overseas populations. These include birds which arrived in pre-European times such as the pukeko (*Porphyrio porphyrio*) and the fantail/piwakawaka (*Rhipidura fuliginosa*). The Maori name for the silvereye (*Zosterops lateralis*) *left,* is tauhou, meaning stranger, and marks its arrival in New Zealand only in the 1850s.

The populations of some bird species that we share with Australia, such as the black swan (*Cygnus atratus*) and grey teal (*Anas gibberifrons*), are occasionally augmented by groups driven to Trans-Tasman migration by drought or other natural pressures.

Close relatives within New Zealand probably mark different arrival times for immigrant groups of the same species. For example, the pied stilt (*Himantopus himantopus*) in New Zealand is the same species as in Australia. The black stilt (*Himantopus novaezealandiae*) may well be descended from immigrant groups of pied stilts which arrived many centuries ago and evolved differently in the New Zealand habitat.

Always there will be new birds to follow the ancient flight path of the white heron. The spur-winged plover (*Vanellus miles*) was first seen here in 1886. It began breeding in Southland in 1932 and can now be found throughout the South Island and the lower half of the North Island. The welcome swallow (*Hirundo neoxena*) was not seen on the main islands of New Zealand until the 1950s. Now it breeds all over the country.

The next permanent settler could well be the Australian colonial neighbour of the white heron, the cattle egret (*Ardeola ibis*). Though they were not seen here until 1963, increasingly large groups arrived in the 1970s and now hundreds make the double crossing of the Tasman Sea each year. During the winter and spring they feed in livestock pastures across the country before returning to New South Wales and southern Queensland to breed. It seems only a matter of time before they establish breeding colonies here.